KING MIDAS

MIDAS REX

A GOLDEN TALE PICTURED THROUGH
TOLD BY THE MIND
OF
JOHN WARREN STEWIG OMAR RAYYAN

HOLIDAY HOUSE • NEW YORK

To Mildred Wilcox Dill,
who understands the gold of love.
J. W. S.

Thanks to King Pop and Queen Mom
for their magic touch.
O. R.

Text copyright © 1999 by John Warren Stewig
Illustrations copyright © 1999 by Omar Rayyan
ALL RIGHTS RESERVED
Printed in the United States of America
FIRST EDITION

Library of Congress Cataloging-in-Publication Data
Stewig, John W.
King Midas / John Warren Stewig; illustrated by Omar Rayyan.
—1st ed.
p.   cm.
Summary: A king finds himself bitterly regretting the consequences
of his wish that everything he touches would turn to gold.
ISBN 0-8234-1423-X
1. Midas (Legendary character)—Juvenile literature.
[1. Midas (Legendary character)   2. Mythology, Greek.]   I. Rayyan,
Omar, ill.   II. Title.
BL820.M55S74   1999
398.2′0938′02—dc21
98-21222   CIP   AC

Once upon a time there lived a king of Phrygia. His name was Midas. He was fonder of gold than of anything in the world, except for his daughter, Marygold.

In earlier days, when Marygold was in a cradle and the queen still alive, King Midas would sit in his garden and smell his beautiful roses. But now he only gazed at them, wondering how much they'd be worth if each rose petal were made of gold.

The king became so obsessed that he could no longer bear to see or touch any object that wasn't gold. He took to spending most of his time in the dungeon beneath the castle, examining all his treasures.

Though Midas considered himself happy, he knew he would never be completely content until the whole room was filled with gold.

One day when the king was admiring a pile of golden coins in the dungeon, a shadow fell upon them. Midas looked up and saw a stranger.

The king had bolted the door. No mere human could have entered the dungeon. Might this visitor be some sort of god? Perhaps he had come to do Midas a favor? What could that be, unless it was to help multiply the king's treasure?

The stranger gazed around the room. "You are indeed a wealthy man, my friend," he observed. "I doubt whether any four walls in all the earth contain as much gold as you have here."

"I have done pretty well," Midas agreed. "But this is merely a trifle, only a small portion of the world's gold."

"What!" exclaimed the stranger. "Then you are not content? What would satisfy you?"

"I am weary of the time and trouble it takes to collect my treasures," said Midas. "I wish that everything I touch might turn to gold."

The stranger's smile grew so bright that sunlight
seemed to fill the room. "You have thought of a brilliant
wish, the Golden Touch. But will this satisfy you?"

"How could it fail?" asked the king.

"And you will never regret possessing it?"

"Nothing could make me happier," answered Midas.

"Be it as you wish," agreed the stranger. "Tomorrow at sunrise
you will have the Golden Touch." The stranger became brighter
still, and Midas closed his eyes so as not to be blinded. When he
opened them again, the stranger was gone.

The next day, before the sun reached over the hills, King Midas awoke. He stretched out his arm and laid a finger on the chair beside his bed. But the chair remained ebony. Had he only dreamed about the visitor?

He lay back in bed, growing sadder and sadder. Soon, a sunbeam shone through the window and onto the bed covering. Midas watched in amazement as the linen fabric changed into woven gold. The Golden Touch had come with the first sunbeam.

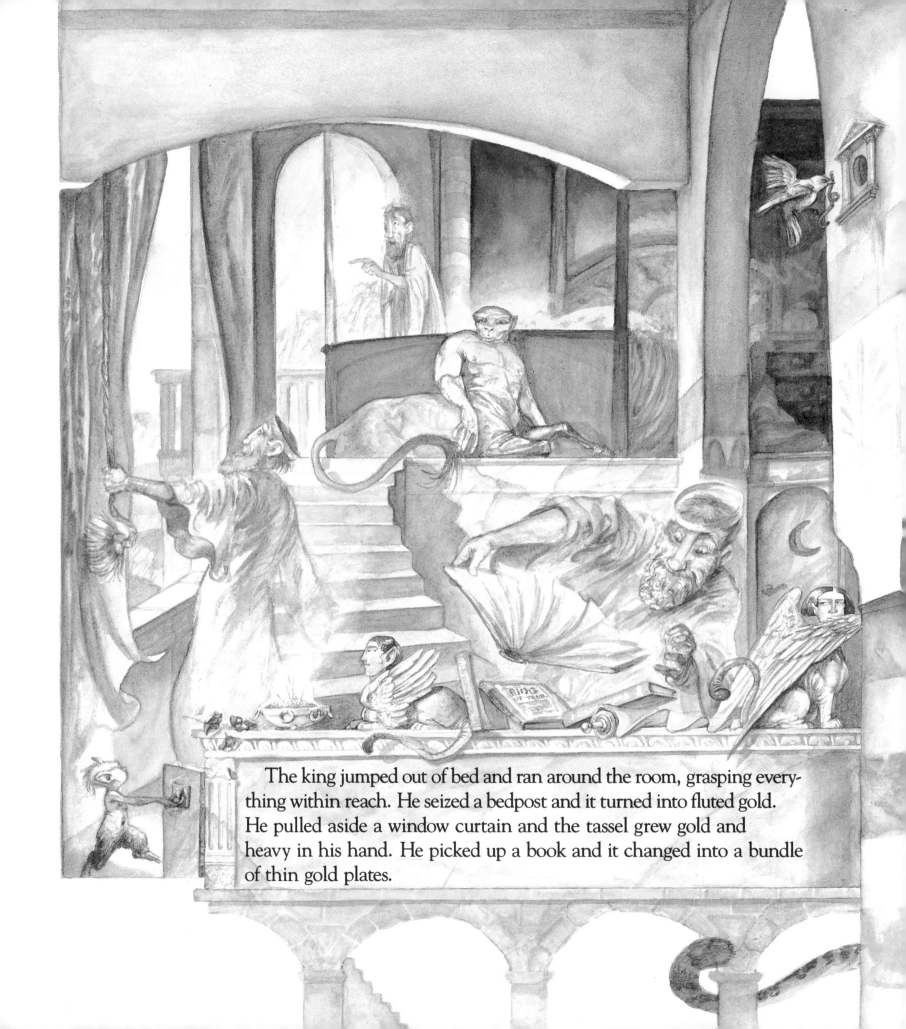

The king jumped out of bed and ran around the room, grasping everything within reach. He seized a bedpost and it turned into fluted gold. He pulled aside a window curtain and the tassel grew gold and heavy in his hand. He picked up a book and it changed into a bundle of thin gold plates.

From his pocket he took a handkerchief that Marygold had hemmed. It, too, changed to gold. But the king wished his daughter's handiwork had remained the same as when she had given it to him.

Next Midas picked up his spectacles. The moment he touched them, the glass turned to metal. This is a bother, he thought. Now I can't see through them. No matter. My own eyes will serve ordinary purposes, and little Marygold will soon be old enough to read to me.

As Midas descended the royal staircase, the balustrade became a bar of burnished gold. He lifted the door latch, which immediately turned from brass to gold, and went into his garden. Here Midas found a number of beautiful roses in full bloom, but as he hurried from bush to bush, touching each flower and bud, even the worms in the hearts of some were turned to gold. By the time this work was complete, the serving maid summoned the king to breakfast.

There, spread out on the table, was a breakfast fit for a king. As Midas adjusted his newly gold napkin, he heard Marygold crying.

"Come here, my dear. Tell me what is wrong."

Marygold held out a rose. It had recently been luscious red, soft and sweet smelling. Now it stood stiffly on its golden stem.

"Father," Marygold sobbed, "I went to cut roses for you. But all of them are spoiled."

"Sit down and have breakfast, my dear. You can easily sell this magnificent rose to buy many ordinary ones."

As Midas poured himself coffee, the pot changed into gold, too. Dining on a breakfast service of gold is rather more extravagant than even I am used to, the king thought to himself. Then he lifted the cup. The instant his lips touched the coffee, it became molten gold and hardened to a lump!

Next he took one of the steaming muffins, but had scarcely broken it when it changed from golden cornmeal into golden metal. Almost in despair, he picked up a boiled egg, which underwent the same change.

King Midas next snatched a small potato and crammed it into his mouth, attempting to swallow it in a hurry. But the Golden Touch was too nimble for him. He found his mouth full, not of mealy potato, but of solid metal. He roared aloud and jumped up, stomping around the room.

Marygold asked, "Dear father, what is the matter? Have you burned your mouth?"

"Ah, dear child," groaned Midas, "I don't know what is to become of your poor father." The king was already exceedingly hungry. How would he feel by lunchtime? By supper? How many days could he survive without starving to death?

These questions so troubled Midas that he began to doubt whether gold was, after all, the most desirable thing in the world. He groaned aloud. Marygold came to comfort him, throwing her arms around his knees. Midas bent down to kiss his daughter, whose love was worth a thousand times more than the gold he had gained.

"My precious Marygold," he cried.

But there was no answer. Alas, what had Midas done? The moment his lips touched Marygold's forehead, her sweet rosy face became glittering yellow, with yellow teardrops on her cheeks.

Heartsick, Midas looked up and saw the stranger standing near the door.

"Well, Midas," the stranger asked, "how do you enjoy the Golden Touch?"

"I am miserable."

"How so? Have you not turned everything you desire into gold?"

"But I lost what my heart loved most," Midas replied.

"So you've made a discovery," observed the stranger. "Which is of more value: the Golden Touch or a cup of cold, clear water?"

"Oh, blessed water," responded Midas. "It will never moisten my parched throat again."

"The Golden Touch," continued the stranger, "or a crust of bread?"

"A piece of bread," answered Midas, "is worth all the earth's gold."

"The Golden Touch," inquired the stranger, "or your own loving daughter?"

"Oh, my child, my child," answered Midas. "I would not have given the tiny dimple in her chin for this whole world in gold."

"You are wiser now than yesterday, King Midas," said the stranger. "Tell me, do you sincerely wish to rid yourself of the Golden Touch?"

"It is hateful to me," answered Midas.

A fly settled on his nose, but fell to the floor like a small metallic button, for it too had become gold. Midas shuddered.

"Go then," directed the man, "and plunge into the River Pactolus, which glides past your garden. Take a vase of the same water and sprinkle it over any object you desire to change into its former condition."

King Midas bowed low to the stranger. By the time he lifted his head, the stranger had vanished.

The king lost no time in snatching up a great earthen pitcher, which in the process changed to brilliant gold. He hastened to the river and, without pausing to remove even his shoes, plunged into the water.

Midas dipped the pitcher into the water and was glad to see it change back to the same honest clay it had formerly been. Seeing a violet at the side of the riverbank, Midas touched it and was delighted that the flower retained its purple color.

He rushed to the palace and immediately poured water over Marygold. She began to sputter, astonished to find herself dripping wet and her father pouring water on her head.

Marygold did not know what had happened, since she remembered nothing after Midas had hugged her. Her father did not think it was necessary to tell his child how foolish he had been. Instead, he led her into the garden, where together they sprinkled water over each of the rosebushes. Surrounded by the roses' perfume and colors, Marygold and her father walked back to the castle.

For as long as King Midas lived, two things reminded him of the Golden Touch: the sand of the River Pactolus sparkled like gold and Marygold's hair retained a golden tinge he had never noticed before. When King Midas grew old, he delighted in telling Marygold's children this story. Stroking their hair, which was also a rich shade of gold, he would declare, "Ever since that morning, I cannot stand the sight of gold, except in your hair."